Everything Is Changing

Carmel Reilly
Cheryl Orsini

Nelson Thornes

Nelson Thornes

First published in 2007 by Cengage Learning Australia
www.cengage.com.au

This edition published under the imprint of Nelson Thornes Ltd,
Delta Place, 27 Bath Road, Cheltenham, United Kingdom, GL53 7TH

10 9 8 7 6 5 4 3 2
11 10 09 08

Everything Is Changing
ISBN 978-1-4085-0109-2

Story by Carmel Reilly
Illustrations by Cheryl Orsini
Edited by Kate McGough
Designed by Karen Mayo
Series Design by James Lowe
Production Controller Emma Hayes
Audio recordings by Juliet Hill, Picture Start
Spoken by Matthew King and Abbe Holmes
Printed in China by 1010 Printing International Ltd

Website www.nelsonthornes.com

Everything Is Changing

Carmel Reilly
Cheryl Orsini

Contents

10th May, 1934

It was my birthday yesterday.
I turned thirteen, and I got three things.

The first was a cake that Mum made.
She had to go next door to use the oven
because we don't have one in our house.
But it turned out all right.
In fact, I think it was the best cake
I've ever had.

The second thing I got was
this notebook.
My dad gave it to me.
He said I will need to use it
to keep track of my life now.

I didn't understand what Dad meant
until he told me what the third thing was.

He had found a job for me.

Chapter 2

14th May, 1934

Today, I started working for a man
who makes houses.
I am really lucky to get a job like this,
with such a good boss.

8

This notebook is for keeping track
of my pay and the hours I work.
But I want to use it to write down
things about my life,
because everything is changing
so fast now.

Chapter 3

23rd June, 1934

We are in the middle of hard times.
Lots of people can't find jobs.
My dad hasn't worked for two years.

That's why it's so important for me
to take this job.
I can help my family
with the money I make.

When Dad lost his job
we had no money,
so we had to move from our nice house
to this one.

It's really run-down –
hot in summer, and cold in winter.
The paint is coming off the walls.

Rats come up from the cracks
in the floor.
They eat anything.
They've even tried to eat this notebook!

23rd June, 1934

Chapter 4

12th October, 1934

When I was at school,
I wanted to leave and go to work.
But now that I am at work,
I miss school.
I miss being with my friends all day.

I also miss coming home early
and playing games with my brother
out on the street.

My work is hard,
and I'm always dirty.
I have to carry wood and bricks all day,
and I can't just stop when I feel like it.

But, mostly, I don't really mind,
because I am learning a lot
about how to make all kinds of things.

Look at this!

Chapter 5

1st May, 1935

I have been in my job
for almost a year now.
I am used to getting up early
and working hard all day.

So far, I have helped my boss make
five sheds, two houses and a garage.

It's hard to believe,
but Dad got a job last week.
After all these years, he's smiling again.

He says the bad times
are coming to an end,
and things will get better soon.

Chapter 6

9th May, 1935

I turned fourteen today.
I can't believe that a year has gone by
since I stopped school.
I don't miss it so much now,
because most of my friends
have started working, too.

A few of them came over yesterday,
and we had a small party.
Mum went next door again
to bake the cake.
Dad went out to buy some lemonade.

23

Chapter 7

30th October, 193!

Now that Dad is working again,
I get to keep some of my own money.
On Saturdays, I can go to the movies
with my friends.

Things are getting better and better
all the time.